W9-BJZ-348

Mr. Tuggle's Troubles

by
LeeAnn Blankenship

Illustrated by Karen Dugan

Boyds Mills Press

Published by Boyds Mills Press, Inc.
A Highlights Company
815 Church Street
Honesdale, Pennsylvania 18431
Printed in China
Visit our Web site at www.boydsmillspress.com

Library of Congress Cataloging-in-Publication Data

Blankenship, LeeAnn.
    Mr. Tuggle's trouble / by LeeAnn Blankenship ; illustrated by Karen Dugan.— 1st ed.
        p. cm.
    Summary: As more and more of his clothes go missing, Mr. Tuggle finds himself wearing a strange
assortment of items until he finally realizes what he has to do.
    ISBN 1-59078-196-1 (alk. paper)
[1. Clothing and dress—Fiction. 2. Lost and found possessions—Fiction. 3. Orderliness—Fiction.
4. Humorous stories.]
I. Title: Mister Tuggle's trouble. II. Dugan, Karen, ill. III. Title.

    PZ7.B61325Mr 2004
    [E]—dc22
        2003026877

First edition, 2005
The text of this book is set in 16-point Clearface Regular.
The illustrations are done in watercolor.

10 9 8 7 6 5 4 3 2 1

This book is lovingly dedicated to my husband, Barry, for his support as I pursue my dreams, and for all the fun we share travelling life's path together
—L. B.

To all the Mr. Tuggles of the world
(and you know who we are)
—K. D.

ON MONDAY MORNING, Mr. Tuggle woke up to a bright spring day.

After breakfast, he put on his shirt and tie.

He put on his pants and belt.

And he put on his shoes and socks.

"Now, where's my hat?" he asked himself.

He looked here.
He looked there.
But he couldn't find it anywhere.
"Fiddlesticks! Maybe I should have
put it on the shelf last night. Oh well,
who needs a hat anyway?"

So he picked up his umbrella
and rode to work without his hat.

At noon, Mr. Tuggle said to himself, "It's such a lovely day, I think I'll eat my lunch outside." That's when the trouble began.

A pigeon flew over his head. SPLAT! That bird made a mess, smack-dab in Mr. Tuggle's hair.

"Jumpin' jelly beans!" cried Mr. Tuggle. "I guess I do need a hat," he said.

In his office, he made a hat out of
the morning newspaper.

He put the newspaper hat on his
head and tied it with string.

"Not bad!" he said.

Later he wore the newspaper hat home.

On Tuesday morning, Mr. Tuggle put on his shirt and tie.

And he put on his pants and belt.

"Well, where in the world are my shoes?" he asked himself.

He looked here.

He looked there.

But he couldn't find them anywhere.

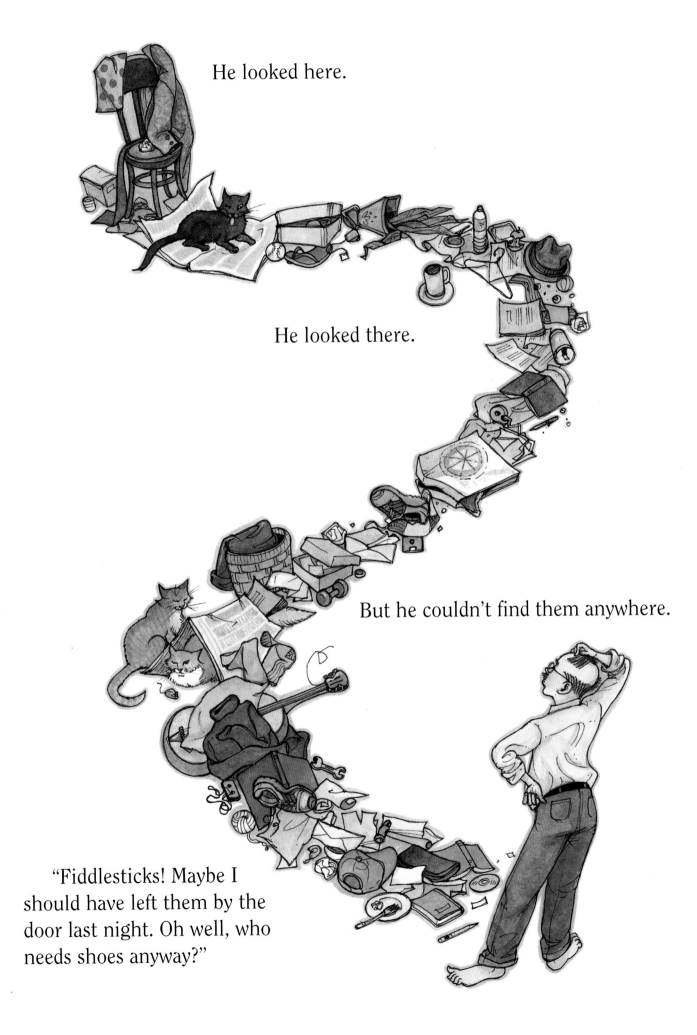

"Fiddlesticks! Maybe I should have left them by the door last night. Oh well, who needs shoes anyway?"

So he put on his newspaper hat and picked up his umbrella. And he rode to work in his bare feet.

People pushed and shoved in the office elevator.

That's when the trouble began.

Someone stepped on Mr. Tuggle's toes.

"Jumpin' jelly beans!" he cried.

"I guess I do need shoes," he said.

He found two cardboard boxes in his office closet and tied them to his feet.

"Not bad!" he said.

Later he wore the box shoes home.

On Wednesday morning,
Mr. Tuggle put on his pants and belt.
"Goodness, where is my shirt?"
he asked himself.

He looked here.
He looked there.
But he couldn't find it anywhere.
"Fiddlesticks! Maybe I should have
hung it in the closet last night. Oh well,
who needs a shirt anyway?"

So he put on his tie. He wore his box shoes and newspaper hat. Then he picked up his umbrella and rode to work in his undershirt.

After lunch, Mr. Tuggle said to himself,
"I believe I need a breath of fresh air.
A short walk should do the trick."

That's when the trouble began.
Bees darted back and forth. Buzzz, Buzzz, Buzzz.
They spotted the tattooed roses on Mr. Tuggle's chest.
"Jumpin' jelly beans!" he cried. "I guess I do need a shirt!"
And he ran all the way back to his office.

Mr Tuggle took down his curtains.
He tied one curtain to his chest.
He tied the other curtain to his back.
"Not bad!" he said.

Later he wore the curtain shirt home.

On Thursday morning, Mr. Tuggle put on his curtain shirt and his tie.

He put on his pants and belt.

He put on his box shoes and his newspaper hat.

"Well, heavens to Betsy, where's my umbrella?" he asked himself.

He looked here.

He looked there.

But he couldn't find it anywhere.

"Fiddlesticks! Maybe I should have put it in the umbrella stand last night. Oh well, who needs an umbrella anyway?"

So he rode to work without one.

After he'd eaten his lunch, Mr. Tuggle said, "I think
I'll go to the park and feed the squirrels."

That's when the trouble began.

Plop, plop, plop. A light rain started to fall.

Mr. Tuggle heard the drops hitting his newspaper
hat. His pants and curtain shirt became damp and cold.
His box shoes started to get wet.

"Jumpin' jelly beans! I guess I do need an umbrella,"
he said.

And he ran all the way back to his office.

Mr. Tuggle noticed a large picture hanging on the wall.
He reached up and took it down.

Later he carried the picture over his head as he walked in
the rain to the bus stop.

A crowd was waiting there in front of a department store, so Mr. Tuggle waited with them. He looked at the reflection in the window glass and could see everyone around him.

"What a silly man that one is," he thought. Then he looked again. "Oh, no! That's me!"

Mr. Tuggle laughed at himself. He was still laughing when he got on the bus. Everyone on the bus laughed with him.

Soon Mr. Tuggle got home.

"Enough's enough. I must find my missing things," he said.
He looked here. He looked there. He looked absolutely
everywhere until . . . he found his hat . . .

then his shoes . . .

then his shirt . . .

and finally,
his umbrella.

"I know! I'll put all my missing things where they
belong," he said to himself. "Then it will be easy to
get dressed in the morning."

When he woke up on Friday morning, Mr. Tuggle felt as cheerful as the sunshine peeking through the window blinds. He remembered his missing clothes weren't missing anymore. They were all exactly where they belonged.

He sprang from bed and danced a little jig. He put on his shirt and tie. He put on his socks and shoes. Then he put on his hat, grabbed his umbrella, and headed out the door. Mr. Tuggle hummed a little tune and twirled his umbrella as he strutted to the bus stop.

He smiled and said, "I found all my missing clothes. Today should be a wonderful, no-trouble day."